A Most Peculiar Alarm Clock

Story and Art by Claire Scott

Edited by Bryan Gillis and Becky Jo

Formatting by Becky Jo

With help from Pat Race

ISBN: 978-0-9997476-1-2

To Miah, Aaron, and Pat

Your guidance and friendship make these books possible.

In memory of Willie Scott

Introduction

This book started a few years ago in Orlando during a teachers' conference. Every day, my mom and I, along with a few other teachers, would head to the hotel restaurant for lunch. One day, a part of their conversation sparked my interest.

"Comics are so hard to read. I can never tell what's going on or which box to go to next."

As an avid comics reader, this statement baffled me for a second. Reading comics came as second nature to me, so I didn't understand why anyone would have difficulty reading them. But, over the course of analysis and mulling things over, I found it clear why some can read books and watch movies but not be able to read comics. It comes down to literacy of the medium.

From a young age, we are taught how to read and interpret the written word. All efforts are put into creating a prose-literate society. Most can understand film just through its high exposure, which then creates a film-literate society; however, when have there been efforts for an art-literate society or a comic-literate society? From my experience as a student, my teachings of art analysis are scarce, comic analysis even more so. It is no wonder, then, that comics are hard to read for many.

From these thoughts, this book was born. Combining my mom's suggestion of turning my short stories into comics with this idea, I started crafting this strange mixture of media: prose and comics, side-by-side. Read the story. Read the comic. Look to the medium you're comfortable with if you're ever confused. Certainly, as a representative said at a portfolio day I went to, I could have made an instructive book on what panel you should read next or what the gutter means in terms of time, but what is learning if it isn't fun?

This book isn't an instruction manual. Not one source can teach you how to be completely literate in one medium. Total understanding comes with time, practice, and dedication. Literacy is up to you. This book is simply a reference tool, one for you to learn from, enjoy, and go back to when something's unclear.

This book is yours. My purpose for it may not be yours and that's okay. Want to just read the prose? Do it! Want to skip to the comic? Absolutely fine! Want to compare the two parts? Go for it! Even though I meant this as an educational tool to increase the number of comic readers, your purpose for this book is whatever you want it to be.

Enjoy!

Claire Scott

A Most Peculiar Alarm Clock

The Short Story

Mr. Kevin Robbins lived on the fifth floor of Bryarsville Apartments in room 56. He was a young man, soon to leave his twenties, and was a junior editor at a large publishing company far from his apartment. Most of his mornings were spent frantically getting ready for work, which started much earlier than when he had woken up. His afternoons were much more stressful, as he saved himself from getting fired. Each time, he explained to his boss that his lack of an alarm clock and the distance he had to travel to work made him late; however, Kevin did this with plenty of behind-the-back eye rolls and a tone bordering on monotonous. Fridays were the only days he'd come to work on time, though he denied it any correlation with the paycheck schedule.

That weekend, Kevin finally found the motivation to buy an alarm clock at the nearby discount store. *Five dollars should be enough*, he thought. Pocketing his spare change, Kevin rushed to the elevator, but then he remembered that his front door never shut properly. That rotting piece of wood was always a hassle. He returned and forced the door into the frame until he finally heard the tiny click of the lock. He sighed and soon after heard a smaller sigh from behind. Confused, Kevin turned and saw a bulging set of golden eyes on a face too small to hold them, staring directly into his.

"Why are you late all the time, mister?" the young girl asked, cocking her head.

"Who are —"

"Grown-ups go to work at eight. Why are you always late?"

"Not gonna answer that one right now, kid. I need to go."

The little girl grinned, "You need an alarm clock, don't you?"

Kevin spun around, wondering how thin his apartment walls were becoming, and if he had been talking to himself out loud.

"What did you say?"

"An alarm clock. Mommy thinks you need one. I don't think I need one, so I'm giving you my old one."

The young girl thrust a bright pink alarm clock covered in jewels and embellishments into Kevin's face. He cringed and pushed it away.

"Thanks, but I think your mother would want you to keep such a treasure."

"No, she wants you to have it."

Reluctantly, Kevin accepted his gift. The girl lifted her chin high in the air and silently paraded down the dusty hall. He stared at the engraved unicorns smiling on the frame. *What is wrong with me? I've just taken a toy from a little girl. How low have I stooped?* Dejected, he entered his apartment. Placing the alarm clock by his briefcase, Kevin rested on his sofa. Twinkling music disrupted him.

"What the…?"

Kevin glared at the alarm clock. To stop the tune, he shook the clock but was interrupted once more. Kevin's phone inconsistently rang due to the number of times he dropped it during the rush to work. Ignoring the current task, he answered.

"Hello?" Kevin asked.

"Mr. Robbins?"

"Oh. Ms. Stockwell. Um, sorry about that whole being late thing—"

"I am not calling about that. Fortunately, I bring good news today."

"Really?"

"It seems that the writer you convinced us to let on is a huge success with young adults. Mr. Heis' book, *Backpacks*, has received glowing reviews. We are very proud of you, Mr. Robbins. Now, if you only came in on time, you might even earn yourself a raise."

"Thank you! This is really a coincidence, I mean, I just got an alarm—"

"Very good, Mr. Robbins. I do hope that I will be seeing you on Monday at the appropriate time."

"Um, thank you, Ms. Stockwell."

"Good day."

"Bye."

Kevin closed the phone in a single clap. He never thought that his first success could come so easily. As he placed his phone onto the counter, Kevin remembered the alarm clock. How was it that it rang right before his boss called? He shrugged and sank back into the sofa.

"Boy, I sure worked my magic on that book."

That fateful event didn't end there. Over the next few weeks, contest winnings, raises, and great fortune bombarded him each time his alarm clock sang her sweet, sparkly song. The fact that it woke him up on time was a mere bonus.

Kevin, though he still lived in a beat-up apartment building, was content. As he relaxed on the brand-new sofa that he bought with his bonus, Kevin gazed at his new possessions. *What a life I'm having.* And then his eyes met with the face of the gaudy pink alarm clock. Kevin's nostril twitched. He left the couch, his arm extended, focused. His hand clutched the child's alarm clock and held it over the trash. *This is nothing, right? I'm a success on my own.* For one last time, he took an empty glance at the face of the clock. One chiseled unicorn wept her demise, while the other was distant and cold.

"Just an eyesore. I can get a better one later."

With that sentiment, Kevin tossed the clock, headed to work and immediately continued to relish in his success. Though he discarded the alarm clock, nothing changed in regard to Kevin's new life. He strolled into every room receiving praise, he met all pennies with their face turned to, and won all contests he entered. After work ended, Kevin swaggered home. He entered the elevator with a gleaming bright exuberance and left it with many elevator patrons in awe. Even budging the door open was no frustrating task for Kevin. Once he came inside, a sight paused his reign of cheer. On the coffee table was the pink alarm clock.

Kevin squinted, "Didn't I...? I thought I tossed that thing."

Once again, he threw the plaything into the garbage. As he rested on the sofa, the stench of garbage shot into Kevin's nose. He tied up the bag and bolted to the trash chute down the hall. And with a determined shove, the trash bag plummeted into the dark oblivion. Kevin turned away, heading toward his door. Strangely, the door held close to the frame. He shook the doorknob until the door creaked open, revealing an unfolding horror. A heavy wind whooshed across the room, sending his documents and cash out the open window.

"NO!" Kevin screamed, reaching for the business documents as they flew through his fingers.

As his hope ran out, a loose document flew through the air. Eyes widened, Kevin dived for it. His arm stretched out. He was inches away! Gravity started to take its toll. As Kevin fell, the paper flew out the window. He landed on the table with a loud crash, while his foot ripped a hole in the pristine sofa. The impact caused his paintings to smash to the floor. He turned his face, focused on his earnings flying out the window. Kevin attempted to get to the window in time to shut it, but it was too late. Nothing was left.

Kevin's eyes heavied and his body ached. Pushing himself up, Kevin staggered toward the window for fresh air. The breeze stung the fresh wounds. He sunk deep into his arms, watching his wealth soar closer and closer to the horizon. Just as Kevin shut his eyes to take in the loss, the clang of empty bottles and metal fragments echoed from the dumpster below. He thought nothing of it. He thought nothing of it until the words "alarm clock" rang out clearly.

"An alarm clock! And what pretty carving too… wasteful punks."

Submerged in trash bags, a skeleton of a man swathed in faded flannel cradled the alarm clock in one hand and a short blade in the other. A split trash bag sat on his lap. Kevin stared at the senior unblinking and gripped the window frame. Before he could shout from his window, the old man hopped over the side of the dumpster and darted out of the alley. Kevin rushed to the elevator. He ground his teeth, jamming his finger on the down button. He could only wish for the elevator to go faster. With a runner's stance, Kevin readied himself for the instant the elevator doors opened. He bolted. Slipping through the crowds, the doors barely held to their frame when he flew through them. To Kevin's left was the man, sitting cross-legged and toying with the alarm clock's settings.

"Hey," Kevin snapped, kicking the man's worn sole, "Give it. That's not yours."

The man raised his head, and then retracted it into his shoulders upon seeing Kevin's gold cufflinks.

Kevin gave his boot another kick. "Come on, it's mine."

"No, no… you see, I… I found it back over there —"

"Give it!"

Kevin gripped both of his hands around the alarm clock. He tugged, rattling the old man with each pull. The man trembled but kept a strong grasp. Back and forth they went. Kevin made the final pull. He flew back, nearly slamming his head on the sidewalk edge, and landed with a hard fall. The old man whimpered, muttering, gasping. Kevin flashed a smirk. He went to clutch his prize to his chest, but it wasn't in his hands. Pushing himself up on bruised arms, Kevin saw exactly where his alarm clock went. His shock was interrupted by the old man's rage.

"You ass… that was a perfectly good ticker."

The alarm clock had shattered. Off were the plastic jewels, the engraved unicorns, the rainbow handle. The bright pink seemed to fade to dying rose. Kevin felt about the ground, searching for something to grip. He found nothing. Slamming his fists against the pavement, Kevin stomped to his apartment building, abandoning the clock along with the weary man who was sniffling heavily and rubbing his eyes.

Once foot traffic died out, the old man stretched over to cradle the pieces of the alarm clock. The pieces became submerged in the layers of flannel and thinned cotton while the man hugged them to his chest. Twinkling music rose from the pile. He beamed at the clock but turned once he felt a tap on his shoulder.

"Eh, buddy," a round man said, "Y'know, I saw how that guy was bein' such a jerk a minute ago. Here. Go down to the mall and get a new one."

The old man focused on the fifty the man offered. He took the gift and strained his head in a deep bow. The other man ambled away without hearing the "thank-you" from the gift recipient. The old man continuously rubbed his fingers over the bill's creases and soft, worn spots. Pocketing the fifty, the man admired the alarm clock pieces scattered on his lap.

"No, good sir," he cheerfully muttered, "this clock is just the thing I needed."

Above was a golden-eyed girl staring down at the scene from a fifth story window. She giggled and skipped away.

A MOST PECULIAR ALARM CLOCK

THE COMIC

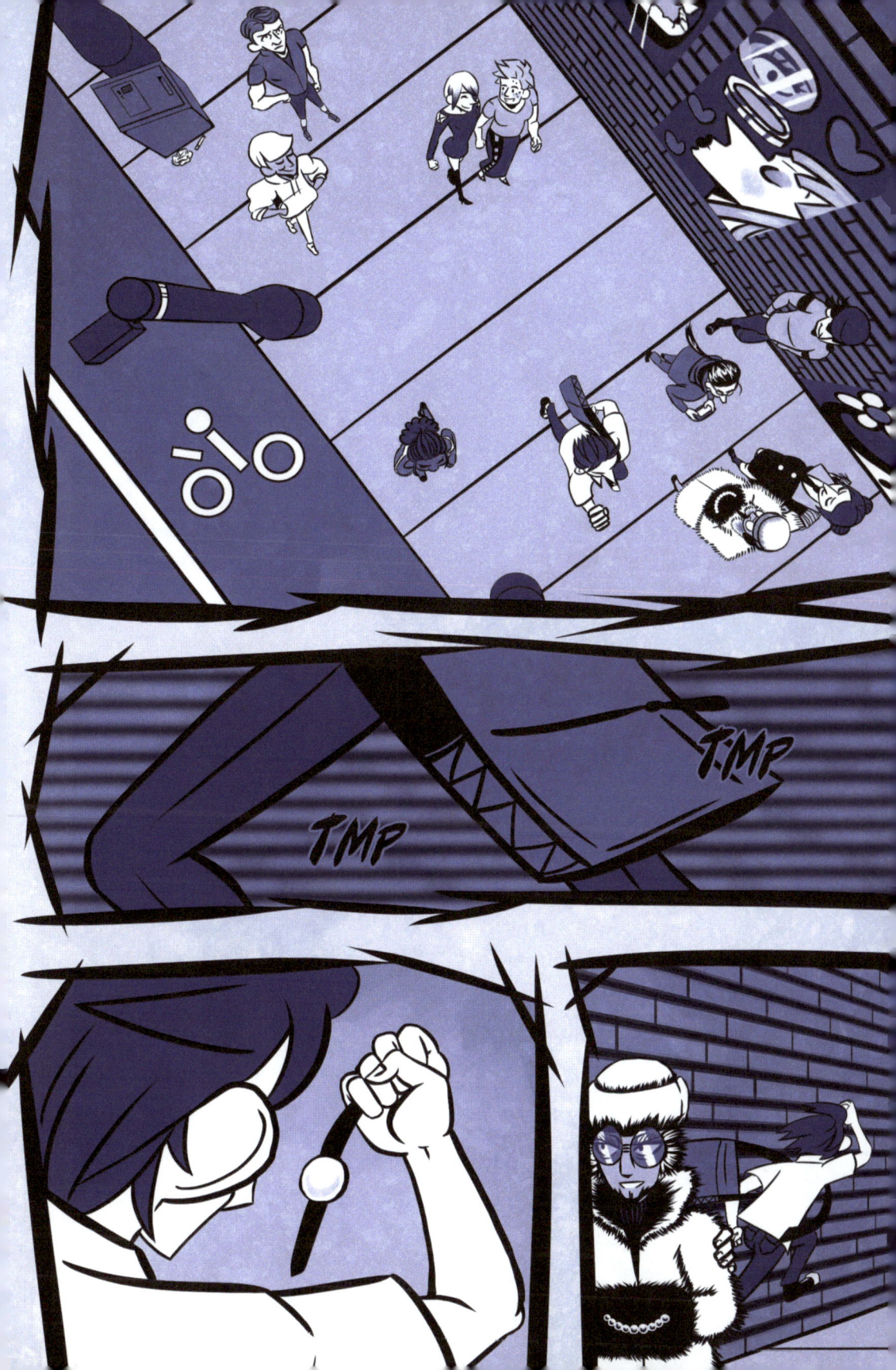

AND YET HIS LUCK
STILL PREVAILED...

AN ALARM CLOCK!

Acknowledgments

Okay. Book 2! It took a lot less time than the first one, but there's still many people to thank for helping turn this concept into what you have in your hands right now.

First of all, a big thank you to the Juneau Arts and Humanities Council for funding some of the publishing costs and art supply purchases. This was my first big project working in digital, so I can't wait to explore the medium even further. Two guys who deserve all the thanks in the world are Pat Race and Aaron Suring of Alaska Robotics. Without them, I couldn't have even started this project. Their hard work and impact on the community shine brightly in this cloudy city. Thank you to all my teachers who have supported my writing and artistic endeavors, especially Miah Lager. Even though I am more than two years past middle school, she still finds time to help me advance my artistry and time to be a wonderful friend. Thank you to my ever-supportive loved ones. Their kind and thoughtful words push me to keep going and overcome any obstacles standing in my way. My uncle, Bryan, has not only helped edit the story of this book, but my other short stories as well.

Lastly, I'd like to thank my mom. She was the one who gave me the idea of turning my short stories into comics. Besides being the best supporter of my dreams I could ask for, she is first and foremost an amazing mom. I hope that these next two years I can make up for at least a fraction of the chores I've put off before I go off to college. I can't begin to say how much her support has meant to me. I hope she doesn't plan on retiring soon, because I wouldn't know where to find a better manager.

Sadly, there's someone who I'd like to thank that isn't here with us. Willie, the star of my first book, has passed away. While I worked, she would always sit by my side, giving purrs of encouragement and being my little quality control expert. Just like in *Meow Cats United*, she was a natural leader and a bright ball of energy. Her presence is missed, especially at times when a nudge on the arm would be a perfect pick-me-up.

Meet the Author

    Claire Scott, 16, is a student author and artist of comics. She
created this graphic novel with financial support from the
Juneau Arts and Humanities Council. She is also the creator of
Meow Cats United, her first graphic novel that debuted in
March 2018. She lives in Juneau, Alaska with her mom and her
cat. She is passionate about continuing to create a voice in the
comic industry and hopes you look forward to her future works.

If you'd like to see more of Claire's work, visit
jccatstudios.wixsite.com/clairescott
Instagram: @jccatstudios
DeviantArt: JCcatStudios

Want to share your thoughts about this book?
Leave a review on Amazon or Goodreads!

Thanks for reading.